大雪大雪快快下！

[美]埃莉诺·梅◎著

[美]卡里·皮洛◎绘

范晓星◎译

天津出版传媒集团

新蕾出版社

送给斯塔西·布朗女士和她可爱的学生们。

——埃莉诺·梅

送给玛丽·B。

——卡里·皮洛

图书在版编目 (CIP) 数据

大雪大雪快快下！/(美)埃莉诺·梅
(Eleanor May) 著；(美)卡里·皮洛 (Cary Pillo) 绘；
范晓星译.-- 天津：新蕾出版社,2016.9 (2024.12 重印)
(数学帮帮忙·互动版)
书名原文：Let's Go, Snow!
ISBN 978-7-5307-6470-1

Ⅰ.①大… Ⅱ.①埃…②卡…③范… Ⅲ.①数学–
儿童读物 Ⅳ.①O1-49

中国版本图书馆 CIP 数据核字(2016)第 206918 号

出版发行：天津出版传媒集团
新蕾出版社
http://www.newbuds.com.cn
地　　　址:天津市和平区西康路 35 号(300051)
出 版 人:马玉秀
电　　话:总编办(022)23332422
　　　　　发行部(022)23332679　23332351
传　　真:(022)23332422
经　　销:全国新华书店
印　　刷:天津新华印务有限公司
开　　本:787mm×1092mm　1/16
印　　张:3
版　　次:2016 年 9 月第 1 版　2024 年 12 月第 20 次印刷
定　　价:12.00 元

著作权所有,请勿擅用本书制作各类出版物,违者必究。
如发现印、装质量问题,影响阅读,请与本社发行部联系调换。
地址:天津市和平区西康路 35 号
电话:(022)23332351　邮编:300051

无处不在的数学

资深编辑 卢 江

　　人们常说"兴趣是最好的老师",有了兴趣,学习就会变得轻松愉快。数学对于孩子来说或许有些难,因为比起语文,数学显得枯燥、抽象,不容易理解,孩子往往不那么喜欢。可许多家长都知道,学数学对于孩子的成长和今后的生活有多么重要。不仅数学知识很有用,学习数学过程中获得的数学思想和方法更会影响孩子的一生,因为数学素养是构成人基本素质的一个重要因素。但是,怎样才能让孩子对数学产生兴趣呢? 怎样才能激发他们兴致勃勃地去探索数学问题呢? 我认为,让孩子读些有趣的书或许是不错的选择。读了这套"数学帮帮忙",我立刻产生了想把它们推荐给教师和家长朋友们的愿望,因为这真是一套会让孩子爱上数学的好书!

　　这套有趣的图书从美国引进,原出版者是美国资深教育专家。每本书讲述一个孩子们生活中的故事,由故事中出现的问题自然地引入一个数学知识,然后通过运用数学知识解决问题。比如,从帮助外婆整理散落的纽扣引出分类,从为小狗记录藏骨头的地点引出空间方位等等。故事素材全部来源于孩子们的真实生活，不是童话，不是幻想，而是鲜活的生活实例。正是这些发生在孩子身边的故事，让孩子们懂得，数学无处不在并且非常有用；这些鲜活的实例也使得抽象的概念更易于理解，更容易激发孩子学习数学的兴趣，让他们逐渐爱上数学。这样的教育思想和方法与我国近年来提倡的数学教育理念是十分吻合的！

这是一套适合5~8岁孩子阅读的书，书中的有趣情节和生动的插画可以将抽象的数学问题直观化、形象化，为孩子的思维活动提供具体形象的支持。如果亲子共读的话，家长可以带领孩子推测情节的发展，探讨解决难题的办法，让孩子在愉悦的氛围中学到知识和方法。

值得教师和家长朋友们注意的是，在每本书的后面，出版者还加入了"互动课堂"及"互动练习"，一方面通过一些精心设计的活动让孩子巩固新学到的数学知识，进一步体会知识的含义和实际应用；另一方面帮助家长指导孩子阅读，体会故事中数学之外的道理，逐步提升孩子的阅读理解能力。

我相信孩子读过这套书后一定会明白，原来，数学不是烦恼，不是包袱，数学真能帮大忙！

　　"起床啦,小瞌睡虫!"妈妈说,"今天是星期六!"

　　我从床上跳下来,冲到窗前。阳光金灿灿,小鸟唱着歌,多么美好的天气呀!

　　可是我失望得要哭了。

天气还不应该这么热呢！现在才三月份。一冬天都没下雪。

我盼下雪都盼了整整一年了。

去年父亲节，我和爸爸一起给我的滑雪板打蜡。

七月四日野餐的时候，我在小山坡上找到了一条最佳滑雪路线。

27℃

感恩节吃火鸡大餐的时候，我时不时地就去看看外面的天气。

10℃

可是新年都过了，天上还是没有飘下一片雪花。接下来的马丁·路德·金日*没下雪。甚至连土拨鼠日*过了也没下雪。

现在转眼就到圣·帕特里克日*了。可是春天哪，你可不能来呀！雪还没下，春天怎么能到来！

---

*译者注：马丁·路德·金日是每年一月的第三个星期一。土拨鼠日是每年的二月二日。圣·帕特里克日是每年的三月十七日。

我看到朋友伊莱在花园里挖坑。他看了看我的防雪手套、滑雪夹克和毛围巾。

"你不热吗?"他问。

我耸耸肩膀,说:"我要整装待雪。"

"杰米,现在外面都快20℃了。"伊莱说。

20℃

我扯开围巾，一屁股坐到草地上。"每年冬天起码要下一次雪嘛。"我说，"我认为这是天经地义的事。"

伊莱说："拍电影时，如果需要雪景的话，人们会用土豆粉当假雪花。"

"那咱们也不能把整个小山坡都铺满土豆粉哪！"我说，"我们要的是真正的大雪！"

"嗯,其实不下雪我才高兴呢。"伊莱对我说,
"我等了整整一个冬天,就想在草莓床插苗呢。"

　　"什么草莓床?"我问,"还有枕头吗?"

　　伊莱听到我的冷笑话,翻了个白眼,接着说:
"我要去买草莓苗了。一起去吗?"

　　"当然。"我看了看晴朗的蓝天,"嗯……我还是
把夹克放回家去吧。"

嘿！我敢说，我们镇上所有爱种花草的人今天都到这儿来了！伊莱直奔卖草莓苗的摊位，我要去看看各种各样的种子。

雪铃花、白雪番红花、雪花荷兰豆……

真是的，他们怎么不卖雪花呢？

回到家,我帮伊莱一起挖坑种草莓。

"为什么要让这些小苗苗间隔这么大呢？"

"它们会长大呀,要给它们留下空间。"伊莱回答,"虽然现在它们还是小苗苗,但是它们会长得很大很大,到了六月会结出草莓。"

嗯。我喜欢吃草莓。

我想,暖和的天气也并不那么糟糕。

可是，不管草莓多么美味，我还是忘不了滑雪的事，尤其是当我的表哥泰勒从科罗拉多州打电话来的时候。

"嘿，小丫头，我今天从坡上滑下来，玩了一整天！"他说，"雪踩上去嘎吱作响！"

泰勒问我有没有坚持练习回转。

"连雪都还没下过呢！"我郁闷地对他说。

他皱起眉头，说："你们那儿没有人工降雪吗？真是太糟糕了。"

表哥的话提醒了我。

"冬日乐滑雪度假村"用一种专门的机器造雪。我们也可以弄一台那样的机器在外面的小山坡造雪呀！

于是我在网上搜索出租造雪机的公司。他们说造雪只要有水、空气和造雪机就行了。

我把页面继续往下拉，哎呀！

气温在0℃的时候才可以。而且，我们还需要很多水，几千万升的水。

那租机器的费用呢？呵呵，这么说吧，用土豆粉做雪花还是便宜得多啦。

0℃

用水量：4千万升

费用：天价

水在0℃时结冰。

0℃

到了吃晚饭的时候,我还不怎么饿呢。

当新闻中天气预报员出场时,我都没有放下手里的事情去竖起耳朵听,这对我来说可是第一次。毕竟春天已经……

什么什么？他说下雪？

　　我抱着滑雪板在房间里手舞足蹈，大声唱："下雪吧，下吧，下吧！"

　　不过，我没唱几句就不唱了，因为我不知道后面的歌词了。

我回到卧室,打开窗户,探出头去。哦! 千真万确,好冷啊。

　　"来吧! "我对温度计说,"加油! 快到 0℃ 吧! "

7℃

我给伊莱打电话。"今天晚上会下雪！"

　　"我听说了。"他的声音很沮丧，"如果太冷的话，我的草莓苗会冻死的。"

　　"哦，不！"我说，"它们还是草莓苗宝宝呢！我们绝不能让它们冻死！"

　　我提议帮伊莱把草莓苗挖出来，放进屋里。可是他说，植物可不喜欢来回来去地搬家。

　　我想，也许这就是为什么它们没长腿吧。

　　到了小妹睡觉的时候,我给她盖上了毛茸茸的毯子,心想,那些草莓苗宝宝会不会正在它们的床上冻得直发抖呢?

　　我们有那么多保暖的方法,那我们也可以给伊莱的草莓苗保暖哪。

　　嘿,等一下……办法这不就来了!

又该刨根问底了。（懂吗？刨根！问底！）

我发现，原来防止植物冻伤的方法有好多好多呢，比如热水瓶泥土保暖法、遮盖法。

甚至还有人用圣诞挂灯做小小的暖气！

我在储物间几乎找到了所有需要的东西。我跟爸爸妈妈说了我的打算，爸爸帮我剪掉了塑料奶桶的桶底。

　　妈妈帮我烧了开水，灌了热水瓶，还给了我一条旧床单。

　　"还有圣诞挂灯……"我说。

　　老爸老妈齐声说："不行。"

伊莱穿着睡衣来开门。

"这是干什么？"他问。

"穿上鞋子和大衣。"我笑眯眯地对他说，"咱们给小宝宝盖被子去！"

我们先放好了热水瓶。

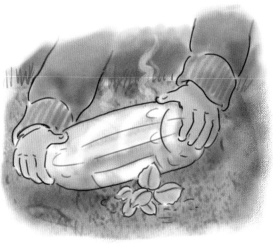

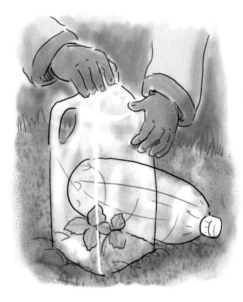

接着，我们用奶桶和盒子把草莓苗一个一个罩起来。

最后，我们用床单把整个草莓床盖起来。
"晚安，小草莓。"我说，"睡个好觉。别被虫虫咬！"

我终于躺到了床上，比平时睡觉的时间晚了半个小时。

　　可我还是不停地胡思乱想，小草莓苗会安全度过今夜吗？晚上真的会下雪吗？

　　我觉得我一晚上都睡不着了。

可是，当我醒过来时，已经是妈妈叫我起床的时候了："起床啦，小瞌睡虫！今天天气可真好。"

我跳下床，冲到窗前。阳光金灿灿，小鸟唱着歌。

大地一片……

"下雪啦！"我欢呼着推开窗户。

我拿过温度计，差一点儿亲亲它，这时忽然想起在一部电影里，一个男孩的舌头冻到旗杆上的情景。于是，我只是亲热地摸了摸温度计。

然后，我"砰"地关上窗户。好冷啊！

−1℃

伊莱已经在检查草莓苗了。

"小苗苗怎么样了？"我问。

他笑着说："它们在暖和的小床里，可舒服啦！"

成功啦！

现在，我终于可以去滑雪了……我是说，从坡上
冲下来。

起初，我还担心忘了怎么做回转。可是当我从山坡上滑下来的那一刹那，什么都想起来了。

伊莱坐着他的雪橇从我身边"嗖"地滑过，他笑得可开心了。

老爸甚至把小妹也带来滑雪了。这是她第一
次滑雪。

雪地真的嘎吱作响！

我不知道自己是第几次爬上山坡和伊莱会合了。
"我要冻僵了。"我说。
"要不要用旧盒子把你罩起来？"他跟我开玩笑。
我笑着回答他："谢谢啦。我有更好的主意。"

不一会儿，我们就坐在炉火前，喝上了热乎乎的巧克力奶。

　　"怎么样，盼了一年是不是很值得呀？"伊莱问。

　　"没错！"我说，"可我还没过足瘾呢。"

　　"还没过足瘾？"

　　"暖和暖和也是滑雪的一部分，而且是最享受的一部分。"我说。

气温记录表

气温大挑战

将一只温度计放到窗外，每天记录读数，制作气温记录表。当天气变暖或者变冷时,气温表有什么变化? 到了月末，数一数，有多少天在0℃以上,多少天在0℃以下。

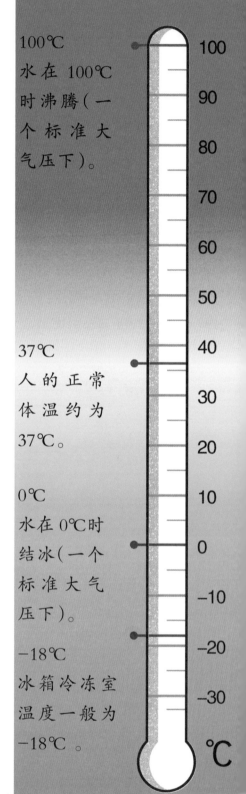

100℃
水在 100℃时沸腾(一个标准大气压下)。

37℃
人的正常体温约为37℃。

0℃
水在 0℃时结冰(一个标准大气压下)。

−18℃
冰箱冷冻室温度一般为−18℃ 。

亲爱的家长朋友，请您和孩子一起完成下面这些内容，会有更大的收获哟！

提高阅读能力

• 请看书的封面，大声读出书名。请孩子猜一猜这会是一个什么样的故事。再问问孩子，他曾经盼过下雪吗？知道气温以后，怎么预测会不会下雪呢？

• 讨论下雪以后，孩子们能进行什么游戏活动。将讨论的结果列成一个表。

• 读过书以后，鼓励孩子区分杰米和伊莱遇到的难题，记录孩子的回答，然后问问他，记录气温是怎样帮助杰米和伊莱解决问题的？

巩固数学概念

● 问问孩子是否知道水结冰时气温应该是多少？让孩子说一说"冰点"的含义。（"冰点"就是水凝固时的温度。在一个标准大气压下，冰点为 0 ℃。）看看第 14 页上的温度计，找出"冰点"的位置。

● 请看第 18 页。杰米和伊莱为什么担心草莓苗呢？杰米想出了什么办法帮助伊莱保护草莓苗？她是如何做的？她的办法成功了吗？

● 回到下雪时的游戏活动表，给杰米和伊莱玩过的游戏打钩。一共有几项？

生活中的数学

● 找一个很大的温度计纸模型，让孩子先看一看，然后标出"冰点"（0 ℃）和"沸点"（100 ℃）。指出这两个点有什么关系。请孩子说一说，当气温上升或者下降时，温度计会有什么变化？如何用温度计来知道气温的高低？

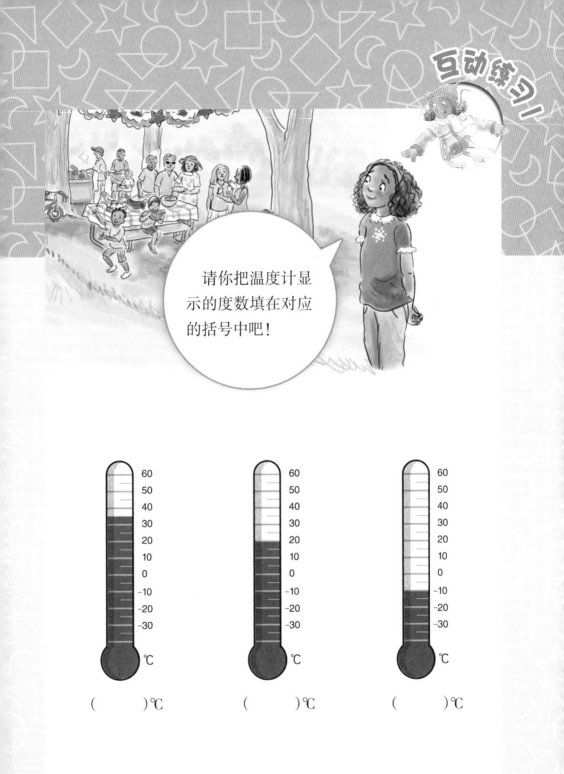

请你把温度计显示的度数填在对应的括号中吧!

(   )℃   (   )℃   (   )℃

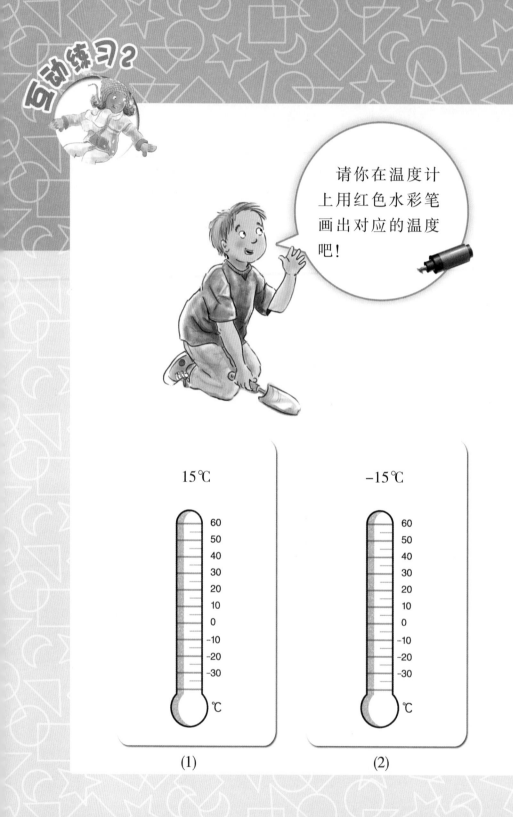

寒假到了，伊莱一家想去温暖的地方旅游。看看下面几个城市一月份的平均温度，哪个城市最适宜呢？请你帮伊莱选一选！

成都
7℃

哈尔滨
−20℃

广州
13℃

呼和浩特
−13℃

上海
3℃

杰米和朋友们打算去郊游。根据下图温度计中显示的度数,他们应该准备哪些衣物呢?用笔把你认为合适的衣物圈出来吧!

夏日里,妈妈为杰米准备了三杯饮料,但是没有告诉她哪杯是热的,哪杯是冷的。请你仔细观察,猜猜它们是冷还是热? 然后,把它们和对应的温度连起来。

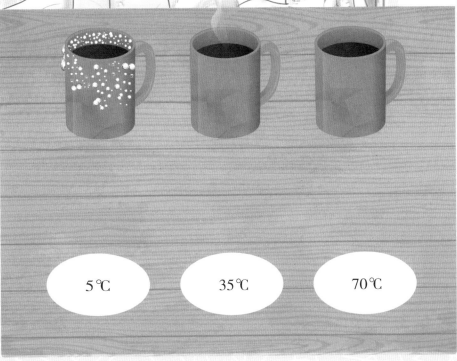

5℃　　　35℃　　　70℃

动物园为动物们搭建了新馆舍，还设置了适合它们生活的温度。可是,有一些动物进错了馆舍,你能把它们找出来吗?

从今天开始，和我一起做小小温度记录员吧！选择三个你喜欢的城市，分别记录下它们未来七天的温度，看看你能从中发现什么。

城市名 日期	城市一	城市二	城市三
年　月　日			
年　月　日			
年　月　日			
年　月　日			
年　月　日			
年　月　日			
年　月　日			

互动练习1:
（35）℃
（20）℃
（-10）℃

互动练习2:

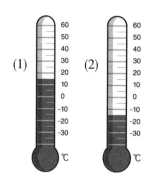

(1)　(2)

互动练习3:
广州

互动练习4:

互动练习5:

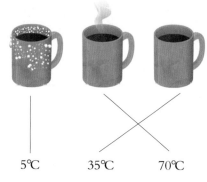

5℃　　35℃　　70℃

互动练习6:
熊猫和企鹅进错了馆舍。

互动练习7:
略

（习题设计:张　青）

Let's Go, SNOW!

"Wake up, sleepyhead!"my mother says."It's Saturday!"

I leap out of bed and rush over to the window. The sun is shining. Birds are singing. It's a beautiful day.

"Noooooooooooooo!"I wail.

It's not supposed to be warm yet! It's only March. And it still hasn't snowed.

I've been waiting the whole year for snow.

Last Father's Day, I waxed my snowboard with my dad.

At the Fourth of July picnic, I scoped out the best route down Sled Hill.

By Thanksgiving, I was checking the weather every chance I got.

But New Year's came and went without a single snowflake. So did Martin Luther King Day. Even Groundhog Day.

Now St. Patrick's Day is right around the corner. But spring can't be on its way already! Not until it snows!

I find my friend Eli outside digging in his garden. He looks at my snow-proof mittens. My ski jacket. My woolly scarf.

"Aren't you hot?"he asks.

I shrug."I want to be ready if it snows."

"Jamie, it's nearly 20 degree centigrade out,"Eli says.

I unwind my scarf and plop down on the grass."It's got to snow at least once every winter,"I say."I'm pretty sure that's a law."

Eli says,"In the movies, when they need snow, they use instant mashed potato flakes."

"We can't cover Sled Hill with mashed potatoes!" I say. "We need snow."

43

"Well, I'm happy it's not snowing,"Eli tells me. "I've been waiting all winter to plant my strawberry bed."

"Strawberry bed? "I say. "Where's the pillow? "

Eli rolls his eyes at my bad joke. Then he says, "I'm going to buy seedlings. Want to come? "

"Sure."I look up at the clear blue sky. "Um...maybe I'll just leave my jacket at home."

Wow, I bet every gardener in town is here today! While Eli makes a beeline for the strawberry table, I check out the seeds.

Snowdrops, snow crocuses, snow peas...

Too bad they don't sell snow.

At home, I help Eli dig holes for his seedlings.

"Why do they have to be so far apart? "I ask.

"They need space to spread out,"Eli says. "They're just babies now. They'll grow a lot before strawberry season comes in June."

Mmm. I do love strawberries.

I guess warm weather isn't all bad.

But thinking about strawberries doesn't help when my cousin Tyler calls from Colorado.

"Dude , I've been out shreddin' the pow all day ! "he says ."It's super crunchy! "

Tyler asks if I've been practicing my carving.

"It hasn't snowed," I tell him glumly.

He frowns. "You don't have snowmakers there? Dude. That's beat."

You know, he has a point.

Fancy ski resorts make their own snow with special snow machines. Why can't we get one of those machines and put it on Sled Hill?

I find the website for a snow machine company. They say that all you need to make snow is water, air, and their machine.

I scroll down a little further. Yikes!

The air has to be freezing—around 0 degree centigrade. Also, we'd need lots of water. Millions of litres.

And the cost of the machine? Well, let's just say it might be cheaper to go with the mashed potatoes.

At dinner, I'm not very hungry.

And when the weather guy comes on the news, for once I don't drop everything to listen. After all, spring is—

Did he say snow?!

I dance around the room with my snowboard, singing "Let It Snow! Let It Snow! Let It Snow! "

It doesn't take me very long, since I don't know the rest of the words.

In my bedroom, I open the window and stick my head out. Brr! It's definitely getting colder.

"Come on ! "I tell the thermometer. "You can do it ! 0 degree centigrade ! "

I call Eli. "Snow tonight! "

"I know." He sounds upset. "If it gets too cold, my strawberry seedlings could freeze to death."

"Oh, no! "I say. "They're just babies! We can't let them die! "

I offer to help dig them up and bring them inside. But he says plants don't like moving around a lot.

I guess that's why they don't have legs.

It's bedtime for my little sister. As I tuck her fuzzy blanket in, I think about the baby strawberry plants freezing in their bed.

We have so many ways to keep ourselves warm. Why can't we keep Eli's plants warm, too?

Hey, wait...maybe we can!

Time to do some digging. (Get it? Digging!)

It turns out there are lots of ways to protect plants from the cold. Hot-water bottles to warm up the soil. Covers to hold in the heat.

Some people even string up Christmas lights as tiny space heaters!

I find almost everything I need in the recycling. When I explain what I'm doing, my dad helps me cut the bottoms off the empty plastic milk jugs.

My mom heats up the water for the hot-water bottles and lets me have an old sheet.

"About the Christmas lights—"I say.

My parents chorus, "No."

Eli answers the door in his pajamas.

"What is all that? "he asks.

"Get your shoes and coat,"I tell him, smiling. "We're going to tuck those babies in! "

We lay down the hot-water bottles first.

Next, we cover every seedling with a milk jug or a box.

Finally, we spread the sheet over it all.

"Good night, little plants,"I say. "Sleep tight. Don't let the strawberry bugs bite! "

It's half an hour past my bedtime when my head finally hits the pillow.

My brain is still buzzing. Will the seedlings make it through the night? Will it really snow?

I'm positive that I won't sleep a wink.

But the next thing I know, my mother is saying,"Wake up, sleepyhead! It's a beautiful day."

I leap out of my bed and race over to the window. The sun is shining. Birds are singing.

And the whole world is covered in...

"Snow!"I yell, and fling the window open.

I grab the thermometer. I almost kiss it, but then I think about the movie where the boy's tongue sticks to a frozen flagpole. So I just give it a friendly pat.

Then I slam the window shut. Brrrr!

Eli is already out checking on his plants.

"How are the babies?"I ask.

He smiles."Snug in their nice warm bed!"

We did it!

And now, at last, I can go snowboarding...I mean,"shreddin' the pow."

I'm worried I might have forgotten how to carve. But as soon as I hit Sled Hill, it all comes back.

Eli whizzes past me on his snow tube, laughing.

My dad even takes my little sister for a sled ride. It's her very first time.

Super crunchy!

I meet Eli on my zillionth trip up the hill.

"I'm getting cold,"I say.

"Should I cover you with an old cardboard box?"he teases.

I laugh."Nope. I have a better idea."

Soon we are sitting in front of the fireplace, sipping hot chocolate.

"So, was it worth waiting all year?"Eli asks.

"Absolutely!"I say."And it isn't over yet."

"It's not?"

"This is part of snowboarding, too,"I explain."The very best part—warming up!"